The Puck Hog

THE PUCK HOG

by Christie Casciano

illustrated by Rose Mary Casciano Moziak

North Country Books, Inc

Utica, New York

ISBN-10 1-59531-037-1
ISBN-13 978-1-59531-037-8

Design by Zach Steffen & Rob Igoe, Jr.

Library of Congress Cataloging-in-Publication Data in Progress

North Country Books, Inc.
220 Lafayette Street
Utica, New York 13502
www.northcountrybooks.com

To my children, Joseph
and Sophia, and my
husband John, who
inspire me every day.
-Christie Casciano

To my sons, Christopher
and Daniel.
-Rose Mary Casciano Moziak

Preface

I decided to write this book because I love youth hockey. My daughter will be a Squirt this year (she may be the only girl on the team again, but that doesn't seem to bother her one bit), and my son will be playing on his high school team. In between hockey games and practices, I work full-time as a TV news anchor and reporter. All this keeps me very busy, but I wouldn't trade a second of it! I hope you enjoy reading *The Puck Hog* as much as I enjoyed writing it.

Chapter One

Sophia was right near the net when she impatiently yelled out to her teammate, "Come on, Eddie. Pass the puck!"

But Eddie ignored the sound of Sophia's stick tapping on the ice. He was a few feet in front of the blue line. You could feel the tension all around as he rolled his wrist back and gripped his stick tightly. SLAP! The puck soared lightning fast into the net as the goalie swooped down. Parents in the stands cheered, "Nice save! Good job, goalie!"

The goalie's big helmet snapped back up, and he slowly raised his glove. It was a shocker. No puck!

"Goal scored by number five!" the referee shouted to the score-keeper, "Unassisted."

Eddie's dad yelled from the stands, "That's the way to do it, son. You're a scoring machine!"

"Make room on the ice," Jack groaned from the bench. "Here comes another Eddie celebration."

Eddie raised his stick over his head and skated right in front of Jack and the rest of the team. He slipped down on one knee and clenched his fist in his glove, "Oh yeah, scored another one!"

Jack turned to Michael, "Gee, ya' think it would get a little old after a while."

The way Eddie was strutting across the ice with his white helmet, white jersey, and head moving back and forth reminded Sophia of a great big chicken.

All of a sudden the chicken was right in her face. "Take notes, So-pheeee. Low glove side goes in every time."

"The name is Sophia," Sophia replied, "and I got it."

Chapter Two

"Check the scoreboard and you can all thank me again," Eddie said as the game-ending buzzer blared out loudly. His teammates all bit down hard on their mouth guards. That stopped them from saying what they really wanted to say to Eddie.

The final score was 10-4. Five goals were scored by Eddie. Jack said to Danny, "He did help make this a solid win, you know."

"True," said Danny as he slammed his stick against the boards. "He made sure we all knew it too. That's what gets me."

Brian chimed in, "He does score a lot of goals. We never won this many games before Eddie joined the team."

Jack added, "Yeah. Have you seen our stats? We have more wins than any other team in our league!"

"Really?" Sophia questioned Jack. She couldn't believe it, because last year they had the record of being the team with the most ties. She hated games that ended in a tie. Her brother always said ties are like kissing your sister. "Yuck," she thought.

"Sure he scores," Holden jumped into the conversation, "but he never passes. He's all over the ice and never plays his position. Sometimes I pretend I'm really tired or my lace has come undone just so I don't have to go out on the same shift as Eddie."

"Remember last year, when we were getting so clobbered by Oswego that the score didn't even matter?" Danny recalled. "We all just kept shooting and shooting and never gave up. Ah, the good old days when we had fun."

"Look," Jack said, "we're doing what we love. We're playing hockey. We're winning. Eddie's part of our team. Coach always says team-mates should stick together."

Chapter Three

In the locker room Eddie's mouth kept on yapping, "Who's the man? Did you all see how it's done? Oh yeah!"

Holden curled his lips into a half smile and said to Eddie, "Yup. We all saw it, Eddie. Congratulations."

"Then put up your gloves everybody. High-five me!"

The gloves quietly went up, and Eddie bounced around the locker room and smacked his glove against everyone else's. But it was so quiet. It was never this quiet after a game. No one felt much like celebrating.

The locker room door flew open. It was Coach Paul, and he was grinning from ear to ear. He stopped, looked around, and seemed puzzled. The dead silence took him by surprise. Why weren't the kids singing, tossing their socks at each other, and trying to turn the locker room lights on and off like they usually did? He just figured they must be really tired after skating so hard. So he added a little extra volume to his booming voice.

"Great job, kids! Wow! I can't believe how hard you all skated out there. We just beat one of the toughest teams in our league. It wasn't even close. Eddie, I think I lost count. Was that three goals today?" asked the coach.

Eddie quickly corrected him, "No, Coach." He held up his fist and raised one finger at a time. "I had one, two, three, four, five!" Eddie folded three of his fingers and he made sure everyone could see the remaining two. "That would be two more than a hat trick."

"Wow! Our amazing Eddie," the coach said proudly. "You kids keep playing like this and we're going to have a season you'll be talking about for a long time, even when..." the coach paused to pull his hat off of his head, "you have hair like mine." The whole team burst out laughing because their coach had a bald spot.

"Now that's more like it, team!"

Brian was the first to run over to the switch and turn off the lights. "Hey!" they all began to yell as Jamie got the music going.

Chapter Four

As usual, Eddie was the first one dressed, and he couldn't wait to collect his reward from his dad for scoring all of those goals. He hurried out of the locker room, all the while wondering whether he would get two or maybe three dollars this time for each goal.

As soon as the coach moved out into the hallway to talk to their parents, Sophia yelled out, "Huddle up! Now!"

Everyone swarmed to the middle of the locker room and stood shoulder to shoulder. Jack got the conversation started: "You know, maybe we should say something to the coach. Like, how we're not having fun and it's all because of Eddie."

A frustrated Brian added, "I know, I've had it with Eddie! Once he has it, you never see the puck again. Did you see how he caught right up to me when I had that breakaway today? So, I pass it to him thinking he'll pass it back to me when I get in front of the net. Never happened. The kid has unbelievable luck too. Rebounds? Forget about it."

"Wow, guys. Listen to us, complaining because a teammate is scoring?" Sophia shook her head, "This is just not right."

Holden spoke up, "So maybe we should say something to the coach."

"I don't know," said Jack. "I heard the coach tell Eddie's mom and dad how excited he is that Eddie's on the team now. He said that, with Eddie, we finally have a shot at making it all the way to the State Tournament in Lake Placid. Coach Paul says he's never had a team make it before and this could be the year. He's so excited about it. We're like his dream team or something."

"Well, he's dreaming if he thinks this season is any fun," added

Brian. "Is anybody having fun?"

"NOOOOOOO," the kids moaned in unison.

"But," Holden sighed, "if we tell him how we all really feel, he'll probably switch the lines and it'll mess up the whole team. After all, we ARE winning."

"And haven't you noticed?" asked Jamie. "Every other team in our league has a big trophy in the case except for ours. This could be our year."

"I guess," Holden sighed.

Chapter Five

She was really curious about the team's stats, so as soon as Sophia got home, she logged onto the computer and clicked on the team's web site. Jack was right. Their team was the hottest one in the league right now. They had more wins than anybody else. They had become THE team to beat. That had never happened before, and she had to admit, it was pretty cool.

"Stats, smats!" Sophia wondered, "So how are mine? And what about my buddy, Eddie? Hmmm. Do I really want to know? Oh, I guess." She clicked the mouse to reveal the players' stats.

Okay, she knew Eddie would have a lot of goals. But thirty? Thirty goals? HOLY HOCKEY STICKS! That had to be a team record.

Jack, Holden, Michael, and Danny had ten, eleven, nine, and eight. Brian? Oh boy, none. Poor Brian. Then she checked her column. She had eight. Only eight?

"Wait, a minute," she thought. "I think the coach forgot about that game in Fulton when I...oh...no...that's right, I passed it to Eddie and he's the one who scored. Eight goals. Guess that is right. Ugh.

"But look at that column. Look at all those assists! Whoa, I've got fifteen assists? That's more than anyone else on the team. Holden, Jack, Brian, Danny, Michael, and everyone else have at most seven each. So, I'm leading in assists! That's kind of cool.

"Let me check Eddie again. Drum roll please as I click the mouse and find the Eddie assist numbers. This should be interesting. It reads? Zero? Zip? Nada? Not ONE single assist during the whole season? EDDIE, SMEDDIE!" Sophia shouted and pounded her fist on the desk.

"Hey, what's going on in here?" Her big brother, Joe, popped his head in the door. "Is ole Eddie getting on your nerves again?"

"I guess you could say that. Look at this, Joe. I just checked the team's stats and I've only got eight goals. Look at Eddie's column. I am so bummed."

"Bummed? Look at all your assists, Sis. According to these stats, Eddie doesn't have any? That's ridiculous," said Joe.

"How is that ridiculous?" asked Sophia.

"Sounds like your team's got a little puck hog," Joe replied.

"What do you mean, a little puck hog?" Sophia's ears perked up.

"Every team has one," Joe went on to explain, "although maybe not so much when you get in the older leagues like mine. He might be able to get away with it now, but if he doesn't learn how to pass and play his position, it'll eventually catch up to him. I remember when I was a Mite, we had a puck hog on our team too. That kid could skate like no other seven year old I've ever seen. It amazed me the way he could fake out a goalie and shoot a puck. But he never

passed. His dad even paid him every time he got a goal! I remember one game, his dad told him if he got a hat trick, he would go out and buy him a two hundred dollar stick. Then, another time, his dad promised to buy him the skates that every kid on the team dreamed about having. He ended up with a lot of goals and the best gear, but he didn't have too many friends on the team. It caught up with him, though."

"What happened?" Sophia was eager to hear more.

"What happened..." Joe continued, "is...he cost us the State Championship. Right at the end of the game, he had a great opportunity to pass the puck to one of our forwards who was right in front of the net. But noooo. He wanted to be the hero and win it all on his own. It didn't end pretty."

"The goalie made a great save?" Sophia guessed.

"Oh, doesn't he wish that's how it ended," Joe went on, "Nope. He tried one of his fancy shots but he didn't have luck on his side. The puck went flying over the net and got caught in the netting way above the boards. For weeks he was known as B-T-L."

"B-T-L?" Sophia couldn't wait to hear what that meant.

"Big Time Loser," said Joe.

"Did he quit?" Sophia asked.

"No," Joe recalled, "but he did keep his head down pretty low for a couple of months. The coach had a long talk with him and his dad. No more gifts for goals. He still plays, and he's actually pretty good about passing now. He still has his puck hog moments, but when they happen, we just remind him about States and say B-T-L. That always makes his face turn as red as his favorite jersey."

"Think that could happen to Eddie?" asked Sophia.

"It could," said Joe. "Maybe you and your teammates should tell him how you feel. Or, at least, tell the coach."

Sophia thought about the team huddle in the locker room and thought maybe Joe was right.

"Now forget about Eddie," Joe pulled Sophia away from the computer. "Let's hit the driveway and take some shots on that net outside. I noticed sometimes your teammates miss your passes. You might be passing too hard."

"Really?" Sophia thought about her last pass, the one that Holden missed.

"An easy fix," said Joe. "We'll practice passing the puck right to the tape."

"I just wish the Eddie problem could be such an easy fix," Sophia said as they headed out to the driveway.

Chapter Six

Later that evening, Sophia slipped her jersey back on to get ready for the team's Syracuse Crunch Night at the downtown arena. It had always been one of her favorite events. She remembered the last time she saw the Crunch play and how inspiring it was to see the players pass and play their positions—the way the game is supposed to be played.

"Hey," she realized, "this is going to be Eddie's first Crunch Night experience. Maybe a dose of Crunch magic will cure the puck hog. Just as long as he's not anywhere near me," she thought.

Sophia's mom and dad got her to Section 12, where the coaches were already assigning seats. She spotted her two best buddies and managed to snag a seat right next to them. Jamie and Holden were already making plans to get the autographs of the team's center and right wing after the game.

"Gee," said Sophia, "A perfect night. Crunch hockey. Nachos and cheese. And...no Eddie."

"Hey, are you guys ready to see the pros copy all my moves?" An annoying voice was getting closer, closer, louder and louder.

"Oh no..." Sophia grabbed Holden's arm, "He isn't. Is he?"

Plop! Eddie landed in the seat right next to Sophia. "What's up, Eddie wannabes?"

"Hello Eddie," Sophia, Jamie, and Holden politely grinned.

"Are these the best seats this team could get?" Eddie rolled his eyes. "How are you guys going to learn anything way up here?"

Under his breath, Holden said to his two friends, "You think by watching the Crunch tonight, Eddie might figure out how passing is, like, really part of the game of hockey?"

"Yeah, right," Jamie laughed, "and maybe I'll get to hold the Stanley Cup tomorrow."

The Crunch did work their magic on the ice, and the kids got to see how important each player was for the team.

"Did you see that, Eddie? Did you see that tape to tape pass?" asked Jamie.

"Yeah. I saw. How lame! He could have gotten that goal all on his own," Eddie said as he rolled his eyes. Sophia, Holden, and Jamie just shook their heads.

It was a close game and a big win for the Crunch. Now, it was autograph time. No big surprise when Eddie cut in front of everyone else in line to be the first one to meet the Crunch's leading scorer.

"Hey," Eddie said to the six-foot center, "you might want to get my autograph. I've got thirty goals so far this season and no one on this team even comes close to me!"

The Crunch star knelt down to look Eddie right in the eyes. "You sound like a pretty good little hockey player, but it sounds like you need to work on your passing and on being a team player. Remember, assists count just as much."

"Yeah, yeah. Whatever. When you're done signing my jersey, can you sign my stick too?" Eddie said as he held up his stick.

Sophia, Holden, and Jamie shook their heads again. Her buddies could hear the frustration in Sophia's voice as she slowly concluded, "Yikes. He's clueless and hopeless."

Chapter Seven

The Crunch night experience got the whole team fired up and eager to play their biggest rivals, the Thunderbirds. Before the game began, Coach Paul asked everyone to stay in the locker room for a couple of minutes. He stepped on top of the bench, clenched his fists, and had a real stern look on his face. He carefully looked around the locker room and announced to his team, "Kids, we need a team captain. Show me something special this game, and you've got it!"

"Captain Eddie," Eddie turned to Jack, "That's got a real nice ring to it. Which side do you think the C goes on?" Eddie asked as he used his finger to make the letter C right below his left shoulder.

"Just 'cause you score a lot of goals, doesn't make you captain

material, Eddie," Brian snapped.

"Well, Brian," Eddie said in a sarcastic voice, "as soon as you get your first goal, then you can come and talk to me about it."

Sophia could tell his temper was about to get the best of him.

"Guys!" Sophia stepped in between them. "Come on. We've got an important game to win. The competition is out there on the ice, not here in the locker room. Knock it off."

The game itself seemed endless. One team scored. The other team scored. Eddie had a lot of shots on goal, but the goalie was by far the toughest one Eddie ever faced. It was if he was shooting against a brick wall. Even Eddie's wicked wrist shot couldn't make it past him.

Eddie seemed shaken. It was as if the Thunderbirds had figured out all of his moves. They put a fast skater on him every time he went out, and—as always—Eddie refused to pass the puck.

In the third period, with two minutes left and the game tied at 2-2, the pressure was really getting to Eddie. His dad wasn't helping any. He was yelling at his son, "What's wrong with you? You're better than them! Come on, you better score if you want a ride home!"

"Poor Eddie," Sophia said to herself. "Imagine the pressure he gets at home. Wow, that explains a lot."

Eddie won the face-off and got the puck right to Sophia. She couldn't believe it when she looked up and saw she had a clear path to the net. She was exhausted, but seeing that net and no one around gave her a sudden burst of energy. She dug her edges into the ice and raced with the puck. She was getting ready to position herself to take a shot from the right side of the net, but out of the blue she spotted a huge defenseman coming right at her.

"Wow, he's big," Sophia was starting to doubt herself.

"Sophieeeeee!" Eddie was tapping his stick on the ice. He was right in front of the net.

She remembered the story Joe told about the puck hog. But then she thought how sweet it would be if that puck went in.

Sophia slipped her stick back and the puck rocketed off the blade. She held her breath as she watched the puck glide and slide perfectly to the bright green tape on the blade of Eddie's orange stick. Eddie flicked his wrist. The puck flew right over the goalie's glove and into the net.

The buzzer sounded. Game over. Eddie raised his stick over his head and began his signature celebration. But then he stopped, rather suddenly, when he noticed no one was watching.

His teammates had flown off the bench and were skating full speed toward Sophia.

"Guys, easy!" said Sophia as she suddenly found herself smack dab in the middle of a team dog pile.

Coach Paul yelled out, "Sophia. Great job, Captain!"

Eddie couldn't believe what he was seeing. He felt as if he had just been flattened by a 150-pound defenseman.

"It should be Captain Eddie," Eddie quietly whispered to himself.

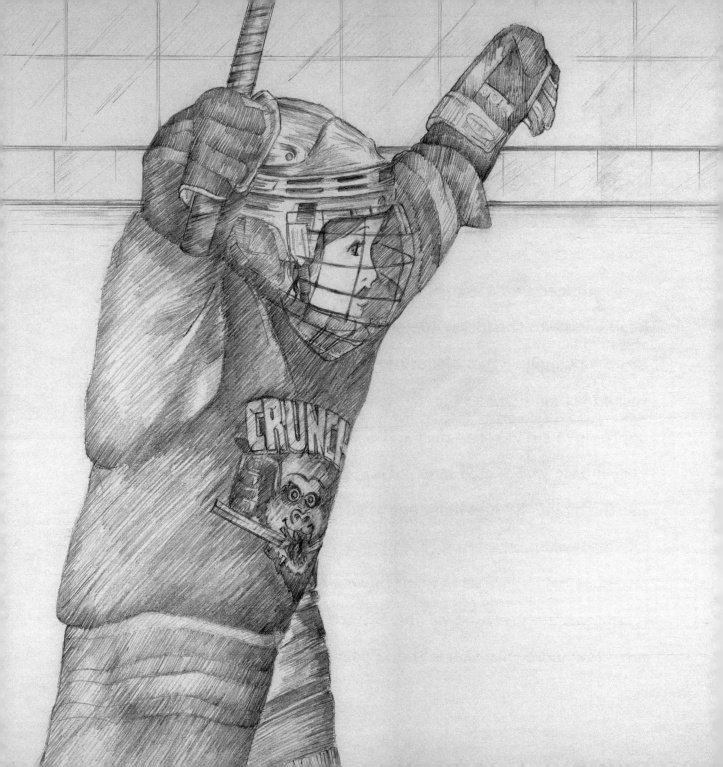

Chapter Eight

A stunned Eddie stayed on the bench and waited for the team to head back into the locker room. He saw Sophia was still on the ice. She was trying to find one of her gloves that fell off when she was rushed by the team.

The glove had rolled over to the bench right near him. Eddie picked it up and skated over to Sophia. He stammered as he handed her the glove, "I...I just don't get it. Did everybody miss my game-winning goal or something?"

"Miss it? No, we all saw it. It was a great goal," said Sophia. "All your goals are pretty awesome. But the whole team could have gotten a few more this season if you passed the puck," said Sophia.

"I don't think that would make my dad too happy," said Eddie.

"Your dad isn't the one out here playing hockey, Eddie. Look how close we came to getting beat today." Her feelings bottled up for months, Sophia was suddenly finding the courage to tell Eddie how she really felt.

Eddie wanted to know, "Then why did you pass that puck to me at the end of the game? You probably could have made it and got another goal in your stats column."

"Stats, smats! That's not why I play hockey. Besides, I wouldn't want to be known as the team puck hog."

"Puck hog? Is that how the team sees me? Not a star? Seriously?" Eddie felt the lump in his throat getting bigger.

"It's an easy fix, Eddie," said Sophia, " It's called passing. P-A-S-S-I-N-G. Remember, assists count just as much."

"I've actually heard that before," said Eddie.

"Well, give it a try," said Sophia, "You might just discover how much fun it is when you've helped a teammate, say like Brian, maybe, score a goal."

"Got it. Captain. Captain SOPHIA. Oh, and one more thing," said Eddie.

"Ooookaaay," Sophia lifted her eyebrows in anticipation, because she was never quite sure what was going to come out of Eddie's mouth next.

"Nice pass right to my stick that got that awesome goal," laughed Eddie. "Fist bump!"

"Just when I was beginning to think there was actually hope for you," sighed Sophia. "Now come on teammate," she pointed to the locker room, "let's go celebrate our win and pig out on pizza!"

Hockey Terms

Assist A pass to a player who then scores a goal.

Captain The team's leader whose jersey displays the letter C.

Breakaway When an offensive player gains possession of the puck and skates toward the net with no opposition but the goalie.

Center An offensive player who takes the face-off and who usually plays in the center of the ice.

Face-Off The start of play. The centers from each team stand at the face-off dot, the referee drops the puck, and the players compete for control.

Forward An offensive player.

Goalie A player who remains in front of the net and is considered the team's last line of defense.

Hat Trick Three goals scored by a single player in one game.

Rebound A puck that bounces off the goalie and gives the team another chance to score.

Referee An official who enforces the rules by calling penalties, determines if goals were scored, and handles face-offs.

Tape to Tape Pass A perfect pass that travels from the tape on the blade of one stick to the tape of the blade of another.

About the Author

Christie Casciano Burns, a television news anchor in Syracuse, New York, had no idea how much her life would change the first time her son picked up a hockey stick. From that point on, she and her husband, John, would find themselves spending many hours watching their children develop their hockey skills. They now shuttle their two skaters, Joe and Sophia, to games and practices at rinks throughout New York State. Like so many other hockey parents, when not in the stands, you'll find Christie volunteering at hockey games, tournaments, and fund-raisers.

Christie is a graduate of Syracuse University's S.I. Newhouse School of Public Communications. She has been a reporter and anchor for WSYR-TV since 1986. She also provides morning news updates for the popular B104.7 country radio station. Christie often volunteers as a celebrity reader at local schools and has hosted events to encourage children to read.

You can follow Christie throughout the hockey season on her Syracuse Hockey Mom's Network, www.thepuckhog.blogspot.com, and become a fan on Facebook!

About the Illustrator

Rose Mary Casciano Moziak is an advertising designer for Spirit and Sanzone Distributors and a freelance artist. She received a Bachelor of Fine Arts degree from Syracuse University. Rose Mary lives in Fayetteville, New York, with her husband Don and two sons, Christopher and Daniel.

About the Syracuse Crunch

The 2010-11 season marks the Crunch's 17th season in Central New York. The Crunch joined the AHL for the 1994-95 season and have had primary affiliations with the Vancouver Canucks (1994-2000) and the Columbus Blue Jackets (2000-2010) prior to the Anaheim Ducks.

The Crunch made history by hosting the first-ever AHL outdoor game (Mirabito Outdoor Classic) during the 2009-10 season, setting an AHL all-time attendance record in the process (21,508).

The Crunch play their home games at the War Memorial at Oncenter in downtown Syracuse, NY. You can follow the Crunch by visiting the club's official website, www.syracusecrunch.com.